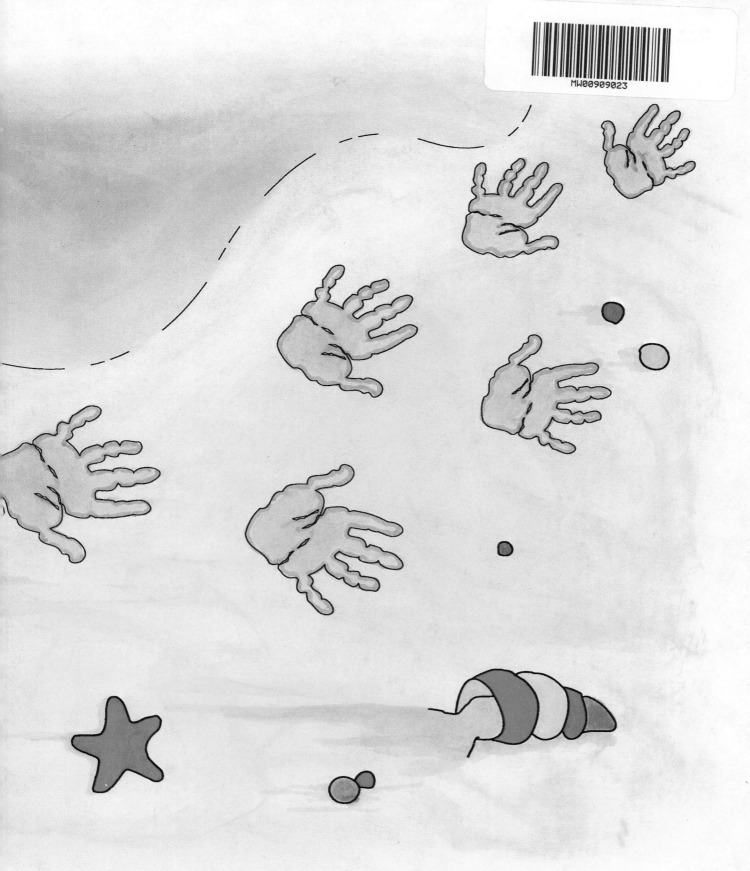

This book is suitable for children up to age

6

Published by Sara's Prints Publishing
A division of Sara's Prints
3018-A Alvarado St.
San Leandro, CA 94577

10 9 8 7 6 5 4 3 2 1

Copyright 1992 Sara's Prints

ISBN 1-881970-00-0

Printed in Mexico

HANDSTANDS in the SAND

Written by Barbara Zamost
Illustrated by Claudio Nalerio

Sara's Prints Publishing

Life is nothing less than grand
When you're walking in the sand.
It's true no matter who you are
The sand is grand, the best, by far.

A policeman named Seargent Gray
Came whistling down the beach one day.
Removed his shoes and thought it grand
To walk barefoot in the sand.

It's no surprise, on this grand day
That everyTHING came out to play.

And in the sand, they left a clue
Of what they are and what they do.
So, when the Seargent looked around
All types of prints were to be found.

As Seargent Gray walked on the shore
The sand showed THINGS were here before.
First, he saw some prints of hands
And followed them along the sand.

But no one walks on hands alone
They'd wear their hands down to the bone.
This mystery perplexed him so
"Whose prints were these?" He had to know.

While searching for what walks on hands
He continued strolling down the sand.
Starfish, shells and a seahorse, too
Washed up from the ocean blue.

Beyond the shells -- not far away
Were footprints left behind that day.
Two big boots had walked the land
And left big footprints in the sand.

Next he came upon a pair
Of web-shaped feet that had been there.
"Ah yes, that's right, I need no hints
I know its quack -- I know these prints."

"It's not a guess, I'm not just lucky
I know these prints came from a duckie."

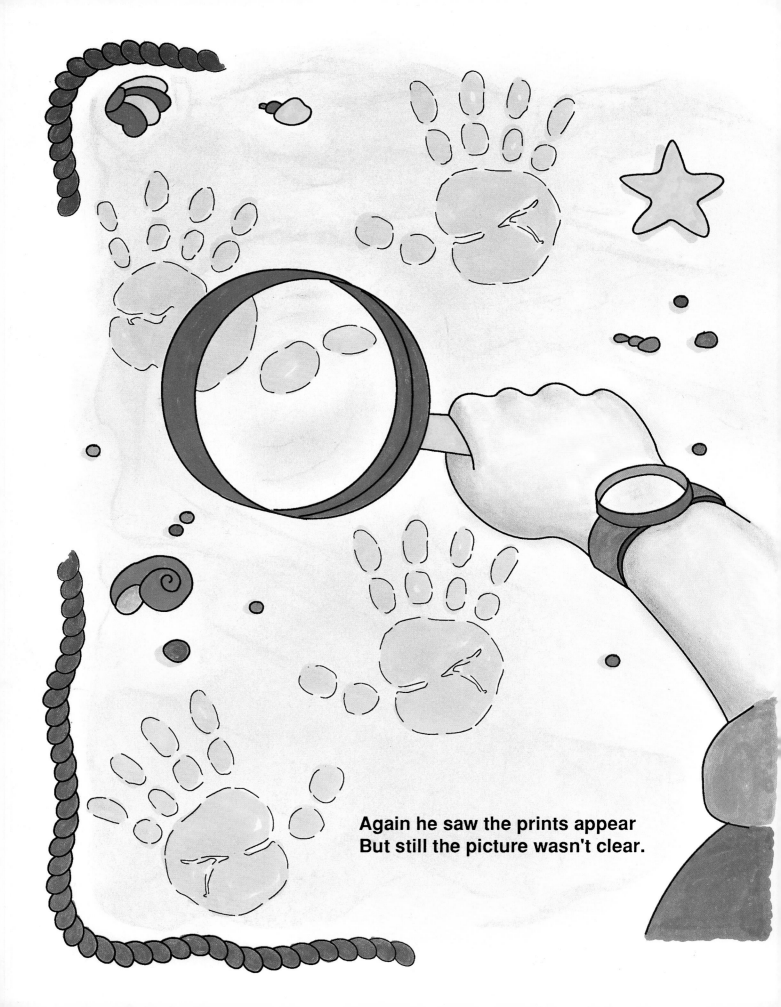

Again he saw the prints appear
But still the picture wasn't clear.

And as he tried to understand
He spied some more prints in the sand.
Their origin was hard to place
Could it have come from outer space?

The ocean is yours. Keep it blue.

It graced our beaches, straight from Mars
And left its prints right next to ours.
This creature from another land
Also liked to walk on sand.
"I wonder if it left here tanned?"

And right beside the martian trail
Were large prints and a long, thick tail.

The Seargent looked at them, unsure
What THING had romped along the shore.
These prints he just could not ignore
He'd seen it in a book before.

He thought and thought and thought some more
"Ah yes, it was a dinosaur!
A dinosaur," repeated Gray.
"What strange THINGS have been here today!"

And circling 'round the dinosaur
He saw a track he must explore.
It swished and swerved and made an eight
The path was anything but straight.

And when he looked up to the street
He knew this print came not from feet.

This mark that curved from side to side
Was from someone out on a ride.
Making tracks out in the sun
Just on his bike and having fun.

But what about those other prints
That left behind no solid hints.
No martian feet, no tail no boot
What creature has this kind of foot?

Before he took another look
He flipped through his detective book.
In hopes of learning what to do
In case he found another clue.

"Now what's this?" said Seargent Gray.
"Has another beast been here today?"

No, he thought. No beast was here.
There was no beast for all to fear.
The circus had just come to town
And brought with it a special clown
Who rides an elephant with ease
And likes to dance and prance and tease.
While riding on his big friend's back
They left behind these beastly tracks.

"I've seen a lot of things today
But these prints will not go away.
I see some more just down the beach
Its owner must be within reach.
It would be nice to end the day
With this one solved," said Seargent Gray.

And as he spoke those words, he saw
A set of great, big U-shaped paws.

12

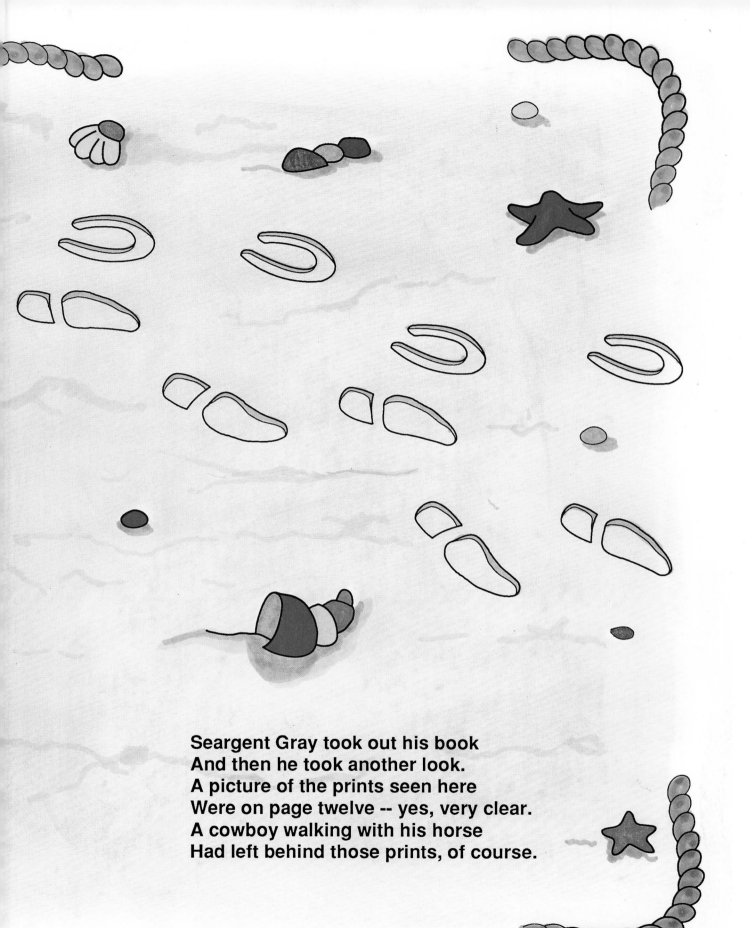

Seargent Gray took out his book
And then he took another look.
A picture of the prints seen here
Were on page twelve -- yes, very clear.
A cowboy walking with his horse
Had left behind those prints, of course.

Just one more print to figure out
"Why am I filled with so much doubt?
It makes me want to scream and shout
And pull each one of my hairs out."

He got a little closer, and
Knelt down on the sandy land.
It was difficult to understand
These feet that looked so much like hands.

"They're hands, not feet, I do declare
Or else, they're something very rare!"

"I'll follow them a few more yards
And hopefully, it's in the cards
That the owner of these prints will stand
In front of me -- here, on the sand."

The prints formed a path that led
To a boy and girl just up ahead.
Laughing as the ocean roared
And the waves broke on the shore.

Sara and Mikey were their names
But their biggest claim to fame
Was the way they walked on sand
Step by step, on their hands.

"Are these prints yours?" asked Seargent Gray.
"Did you leave these prints today?"

"Yes, it's true, we must confide.
 Yes, they're ours," they said with pride.

Still, the Seargent wondered why
Their feet were wet, their hands were dry.
And why, he could not understand
They were not standing on their hands.

"Oh, we just took a break," they said.
"To bring the blood back from our heads.
But, now we're ready for some fun
And finish walking in the sun."

They thought it nothing less than dandy
To get their hands all wet and sandy.
And make their way along the land
Doing handstands in the sand.